First American Edition.
Copyright © 1997 Disney Enterprises, Inc.
All rights reserved under international copyright
conventions. Published in the United States by
Grolier Enterprises Inc., Danbury, Connecticut.
Originally published in Denmark by
Egmont Gruppen, Copenhagen.

ISBN: 0-7172-8767-X

Manufactured in the United States of America.

A   B   C   D   1   2   3   4

PUMBAA
RUNS AWAY
FROM HOME

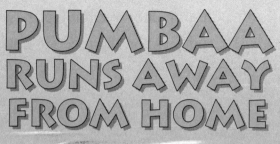

GROLIER
BOOK CLUB EDITION

Simba the lion cub loved living in the forest with his friends, Timon the meerkat and Pumbaa the warthog.

One day, when they were playing on a nearby river bank, Simba found a nut that had fallen from one of the tall trees. He started to bat the nut back and forth between his front paws.

"Gee, Simba, that looks like fun," said Timon. "Can I try?"

Simba rolled the nut over to Timon. Just then,
another nut fell near Pumbaa. "Come on, Pumbaa,"
Timon said. "You can play, too."

Pumbaa tried to roll the nut with his hoof, but
he didn't know what to do next.

"I'm not sure what to
do, either," said Timon.

"I don't think this is
much fun, anyway,"
said Pumbaa, who
was suddenly
feeling grumpy.

"Roll the nut between your
hooves," Simba explained, "but
don't let it get away from you."

Timon tried to follow what Simba had said, but he couldn't seem to get it right. Finally, the meerkat gave the nut a solid kick. Unfortunately, it flew past his other foot.

The nut sailed into the air and hit Pumbaa on the head with a loud KLUNK!

"Owww!" cried Pumbaa, pretending to be hurt.
"You almost broke my head!"

"Don't be silly, Pumbaa," said Simba, pointing to
the nut. "That didn't hurt you. Your head broke the
nut in half!"

Pumbaa kept on moaning and rubbing his head.
But he looked so funny that his friends started to laugh.

"I don't see what's so funny," Pumbaa muttered.

"I told you that game was no fun," Pumbaa continued. "I'm going to get something to eat, instead."

Timon and Simba hadn't meant to make their friend angry. "Good idea," said Simba. "Let's all go."

They followed Pumbaa to the river bank. He looked around for a place where the ground was wet. That's where he usually found the juiciest bugs.

Soon Pumbaa came to a big log. The best bugs always hid in and around wood. Pumbaa carefully lifted the log with his snout. Sure enough—there was a big fat grub.

The warthog opened his mouth, but just as he was about to gobble up the grub, Timon's paw darted out. He snatched Pumbaa's snack.

"Yummy!" said Timon, examining the tasty morsel. "Thank you for lifting the log for me."

Then, with a slurp and a gulp, the grub was gone!

"That was *my* grub!" Pumbaa cried, his tummy rumbling. It felt more empty now than it had a few seconds before.

"If it was *yours*," said Timon, "why is it in *my* stomach?"

"It was mine! I found it!" yelled Pumbaa. "You stole it."

"You didn't find it and it wasn't yours," said Timon. "All you did was lift the log. You didn't know if there was anything under it. I found the grub and I ate it."

"Pumbaa! Timon!" said Simba. "Stop arguing. It's too hot to fight."

"You're right, Simba," said Pumbaa. "I'm going to take a nap."

Pumbaa headed for his favorite spot, where the ground was soft and shaded by a big tree.

But, to Pumbaa's astonishment, Timon got there first! He could not believe that Timon was stretching out in *his* shady spot!

Simba could see that his friends were about to argue again. "Timon," he said, "why not let Pumbaa have his spot? You got the grub, so let him lie down and rest."

"I got here first," Timon said stubbornly.

"Come on, Timon," Simba insisted.

"Well…okay," Timon said, getting up for Pumbaa.

"We can play while Pumbaa rests," said Simba.

"How about that game, *What Am I?*" Timon suggested. "You go first."

The cub thought for a moment. Then he lifted a front leg so that it dangled in front of his nose.

"Hurry up, Timon," said Simba. "What am I?"

"An elephant!" Timon guessed.

"You got it," said Simba. "Now it's your turn."

All the while, Pumbaa watched his friends play and felt sad. "Why didn't they ask me to play?" he wondered. "Maybe they don't like me anymore."

"This one will be easy," Timon said, pushing out his stomach as far as he could.

Then Timon started to make slurping noises. "Take a guess, Simba," he said as he walked around, bumping into things.

Then Simba realized that Timon was imitating Pumbaa. Unfortunately, Pumbaa caught on, too.

"You're mimicking me!" Pumbaa cried, jumping up.

"Right!" said Timon, laughing at his own silliness.

Even though the imitation was funny, Simba tried not to laugh. He knew that Pumbaa was really upset now.

"That's it!" Pumbaa announced. "I've had enough of you two."

"But, Pumbaa...," Simba started to say.

"I'm out of here," Pumbaa interrupted as he walked away. "I'll find some new friends—friends who like me."

Simba and Timon didn't know what to say as they watched Pumbaa leave. "Why was he so angry?" Timon asked. "We were only playing a game."

"Maybe he was just hot or tired," said Simba. "Maybe he was having a bad day." "He'll come back when he's hungry," Timon said, hoping he was right. Simba nodded, but he wasn't so sure. He had never seen Pumbaa that angry before.

Pumbaa walked for a long time without meeting any new friends. Finally, he saw three young giraffes. "Can I play with you?" Pumbaa called to them.

The giraffes were happy to have a new playmate. Pumbaa joined them as they raced across the savanna. But it was difficult for Pumbaa to keep up with the giraffes. Because of their long legs, they ran much faster than he could.

When they came to some trees, the giraffes stretched their long necks and began to chew the sweet-tasting leaves.

Poor Pumbaa tried to stretch. But he was too short to reach the high branches.

"I'm not really hungry," he fibbed as his tummy began to rumble.

Meanwhile, Simba and Timon could not stop thinking about their friend. "I hope Pumbaa is safe," Timon said quietly.

"Don't worry. Pumbaa can take care of himself," Simba said. But he wasn't sure.

The giraffes had to leave when their mother called them, so Pumbaa continued to look for other friends.

Soon he met some gazelles. "Can I play with you?" he asked them.

"Humph!" snorted one of the gazelles.

"We wouldn't dream of being seen with…" chimed in a second.

"…a warthog!" said the third. And they bounded away with their noses in the air.

Pumbaa was feeling very
sorry for himself when he
heard strange sounds.
"Yip, Yip!" He looked
around to find a baby
hyena. "Maybe he'll play
with me," Pumbaa thought.

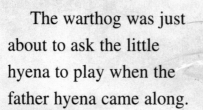

The warthog was just
about to ask the little
hyena to play when the
father hyena came along.

The big hyena didn't look as if
he wanted to play at all.
He looked hungry!
"Ah, I'd better go now,"
Pumbaa said, running
away as fast as
he could.

"Whew! It's a good thing I got out of there in time," Pumbaa said. But there was no one to hear him.

Pumbaa looked around to get his bearings. Then he realized that the sun was setting. "It will be dark soon," he thought. "I want to go home…but I don't know which way to go."

Pumbaa decided to spend the night in a stand of trees he could see in the distance. "Finding my way home will be easier in daylight," he thought.

When Pumbaa got to the trees, he found a place to sleep. "This isn't as comfortable as my own bed," he thought as his eyelids began to droop. "It's cold and I'm still hungry. Most of all, I miss my friends."

Before he fell asleep, Pumbaa looked up at the moon. "Good night," he whispered.

At the same moment, Simba and Timon were getting ready to go to sleep. "Do you think Pumbaa can see the moon?" Timon asked.

"I'm sure he can," said Simba.

"I miss him," said Timon sadly. "It's not the same without him."

"As soon as it's light," said Simba, "let's find Pumbaa and bring him home."

Early the next morning, Pumbaa woke up with the sun shining in his eyes. He stretched and yawned. "Simba! Timon!" he called out. "I'm hungry. Let's get something…" Just then, he was interrupted by chattering sounds and suddenly remembered—Timon and Simba were far away. When he looked up, he saw a group of monkeys playing in the trees above him.

"Hi," said Pumbaa. "Can I play, too?"

At about the same time, Simba was waking up. Just as Pumbaa had done, the cub stretched and yawned. "Wake up, Timon," he said, shaking his friend.

Timon rubbed his eyes. "What's up?" he asked, stretching and yawning, too.

"Don't you remember? We've got to find Pumbaa," Simba said.

Pumbaa had a great time with the monkeys and they liked playing with him, too. They chattered happily as they swung from vine to vine and from branch to branch.

Every now and then, they used Pumbaa's tummy as a trampoline. But he didn't mind. The monkeys were his friends.

One of the monkeys even stopped to pick some berries for Pumbaa.

Meanwhile, Timon followed Simba as the cub sniffed out Pumbaa's trail. In spots where the ground was soft, they could make out Pumbaa's hoofprints.

When they reached the savanna, they met three young giraffes. Simba asked if they had seen Pumbaa. The giraffes told him about the warthog they had met the day before.

While Timon and Simba
continued their search, Pumbaa watched the
monkeys swinging through the air.

"That looks like fun," he said. "I think I'll try it."

Nearby a huge tree arched up into the sky. "I'm
sure I can climb that tree," Pumbaa told the monkeys.

The monkeys chattered and laughed as they
watched the warthog try to climb the tree. It wasn't
easy for Pumbaa, but he kept climbing higher
and higher.

As Simba and Timon tracked Pumbaa across
the savanna, they met some gazelles. Timon started
to ask if they had seen his friend, but the gazelles
ignored him.

Next, the two friends came across the hungry
hyenas.

"We'd better get out of here fast!" said Simba.

They ran away, heading for a stand of trees in
front of them.

The two friends rested among the trees and wondered what Pumbaa was doing. They could never have imagined what their friend was up to.

The warthog had climbed up the tree as far as he could. "Now I'm going to swing like you do," he called to the monkeys.

Then he grabbed a vine and swung out into
the air. Suddenly the vine snapped.

"Watch out!" cried the monkeys.

"Whoooaa!"
cried Pumbaa as
he crashed through
the trees. He used all
four legs, but he couldn't
grab onto anything to
stop his fall.

Fortunately, he got
caught in a tangle of vines
just before he hit the ground.

Pumbaa tried to get free, but the more he
struggled to get untangled, the more tangled
the vines became. "Help!" he cried to
the monkeys. They jumped around,
trying to figure out what to do.
No wonder they were confused;
they had never seen a warthog
tangled in vines before!

In the distance, Timon and Simba heard Pumbaa's cry for help. They ran toward his voice. "We're coming, Pumbaa!" they yelled.

When they found their friend, they just stared in shock as he dangled in the twisted vines.

"Oh, Pumbaa!" Simba said. "How are we going to get you out of there?"

"Simba! Timon!" Pumbaa shouted happily. "I'm so glad to see you."

"Hold on, Pumbaa," said Simba. "I have an idea."

Simba asked the monkeys to pull away the tangled vines, one by one.

"I'm sorry, Pumbaa," Timon called up to his friend. "I'll never take a grub from you again. You can have the fattest, juiciest worms, too. And—you can keep the shady spot. And—"

"Look out, Timon," Simba said. "I wouldn't stand right under Pumbaa, if I were you."

Timon looked at Simba and then glanced up at Pumbaa. The meerkat jumped aside—just in time to get out from under the falling warthog.

Pumbaa hit the ground with a thump. A second sooner and he would have landed on Timon with a thump.

Timon jumped onto Pumbaa's back before the
warthog could stand up. "Oh, Pumbaa!" Timon
said, hugging his friend. "I'm so happy to see
you're all right."

"It's a good thing we got here when we did,"
said Simba.

"If we hurry, we can get home and play while
there's still daylight," said Timon.

The monkeys gathered around Pumbaa to say
good-bye.

"We live in the forest near the river," Pumbaa
told them. "Why don't you come and visit us
sometime. We can all play together."

The monkeys chattered and squealed with
delight. Pumbaa understood that they were
accepting his invitation.

The three friends retraced their steps across the savanna, toward the river and the forest.

"I'm never, never going to leave home again," Pumbaa told his friends.

Before long they arrived at the river bank. The sun was still shining, so they began to play. They frolicked and laughed and enjoyed one another's company.

After a while, Timon decided to try to catch a worm. Simba and Pumbaa laughed at his unusual "fishing" technique.

Later when the sun began to set and the shadows
grew long, Timon offered Pumbaa a fat juicy worm.
"Look what I got for you," he said.

"Thank you," Pumbaa said with a smile.

"Come on, you guys," said Simba. "It's time to
go to bed."

Timon and Pumbaa both spied a particularly
inviting spot near a tree—and raced for it!

Timon *did* get there first, but Pumbaa was right behind him!

"Oh, my!" said Simba as Pumbaa sat on Timon. "I think there's room for all of us, if we squeeze a little bit."

Soon the three friends were sound asleep, happy to be together again.